tana hoban

circles, triangles and squares

macmillan publishing co., inc.
new york
collier macmillan publishers
london

Macmillan Publishing Co., Inc., 866 Third Avenue, New York, N.Y. 10022
Collier-Macmillan Canada Ltd.
Printed in the United States of America

10 9 8 7 6 5 4 3 2

Library of Congress Cataloging in Publication Data
Hoban, Tana.   Circles, triangles, and squares.
1. Circle—Juvenile literature.   2. Triangle—Juvenile literature.
3. Square—Juvenile literature. (1. Circle.   2. Triangle.   3. Square)   I. Title.
QA484.H6   516'.22   72-93305   ISBN 0-02-744830-4

for Heskel M. Haddad
who cares for an eye

NON FLAMMABLE
21105
TA-31308
OUR LIGHTS ARE ALWAYS
ON FOR SAFETY.

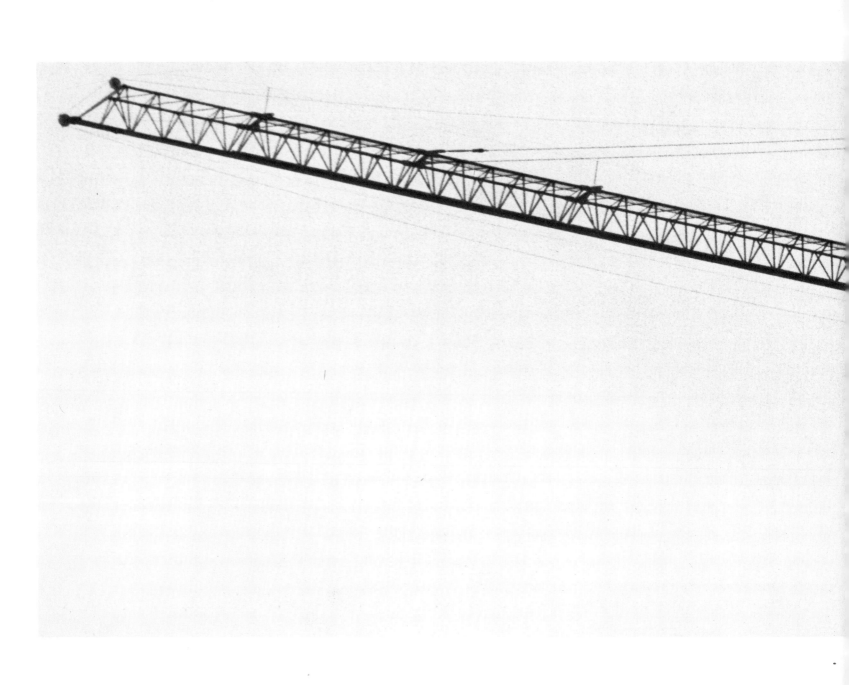